Pinkalicious®

Pink or Treat!

HARPER
An Imprint of HarperCollinsPublishers

by Victoria Kann

For all the children who have missed
Halloween because of the weather.
—V.K.

The author gratefully acknowledges
the artistic and editorial contributions
of Laura Mayes and Natalie Engel.

Pinkalicious: Pink or Treat!
Copyright © 2013 by VBK, Co.
PINKALICIOUS and all related logos and characters are trademarks of Victoria Kann
Used with permission.
Based on the HarperCollins book *Pinkalicious*
written by Victoria Kann and Elizabeth Kann, illustrated by Victoria Kann
a division of HarperCollins Publishers, 195 Broadway, New York, NY 10007.
www.harpercollinschildrens.com

Library of Congress catalog card number: 2013931023
ISBN 978-0-06-302943-9

Book design by Kirsten Berger
21 22 23 24 25 IMG 10 9 8 7 6 5 4 3 2 1
❖
First hardcover edition, 2021
Previously published in paperback

I was going to be Pinkagirl for Halloween, the most pinkerrific superhero in Pinkville! My costume was so pinkatastic, I could hardly wait to go trick-or-treating!

When I woke up in the morning, I went to turn on my light but it wouldn't go on. Then I couldn't hear the radio Mommy and Daddy always played in the kitchen while they made breakfast. Something spooky was definitely happening.

"What's going on?" I asked when I went downstairs for breakfast.

Peter couldn't wait to tell me. "There was a big storm last night and everyone lost power," he said. "I thought the howling was a scary ghost getting ready for Halloween, but Mommy says it was just the wind!"

"Wow!" I said. "Pinkville has no electricity? This is going to make trick-or-treating even better!"

"Hold on," said Daddy. He took out the batteries we kept in the emergency kit and popped them in a little radio. "There," he said, switching it on. "Let's find out what's happening."

The mayor's voice came over the radio. "The electric company is working hard to turn the power back on, but it could take hours," she said. "If the lights don't come back on by evening, I ask that no one goes out trick-or-treating tonight."

"Wait." I gasped. "Did the mayor just say what I think she said?"

"I'm afraid so," said Mommy. "Looks like Halloween will be canceled."

"That's not fair!" Peter and I cried. "Halloween only comes once a year!"

"But the storm is over," I said. "The sun is out!"

"We know you're disappointed," said Daddy, "but if it's completely dark out tonight, it won't be safe to go door-to-door."

"No trick-or-treating?" I sighed. "No candy? This is the scariest Halloween EVER!"

I went back up to my room. My Pinkagirl costume was still on my chair, all ready for me to put on and save the day. But this was a problem even a hero like Pinkagirl couldn't solve. If the power didn't come back on, there was no way I could save Halloween. Unless . . .

I put on my costume and raced back downstairs.
"Hold everything," I said. "I have an idea!"
I told my family my plan.
"It'll never work, Pinkalicious," said Peter.
"Maybe not," I said, "but I've got to try!"

Mommy smiled. "Okay, Pinkagirl. You can give it a try. I'll be your trusty sidekick for this mission."

Outside, Pinkville looked completely different from the day before. People's lawns were covered with leaves and branches that the storm had knocked down. Everyone was out clearing the streets and sidewalks.

Mommy and I zoomed down to Town Hall. "This is a job for Pinkagirl!" I said.

I knocked on the mayor's door.

"I'm sorry to bother you, but this is really important," I said. "Please don't cancel Halloween. All the children in Pinkville would be really disappointed. We have all waited three hundred and sixty-four days for it to happen. I have an idea about how we could save it."

"Really?" said the mayor. "Then I want to hear it. As long as there's a way to keep things safe for everyone once the sun goes down, I promise I'll think about it."

I told her what I was thinking. A big smile broke out on the mayor's face.

"You know, that just might work," she said.

We followed the mayor to her radio broadcast room, which was powered by an emergency generator.

"This just in," said the mayor into the microphone. "There's a new way to celebrate Halloween today. Here to tell you all about it is Pinkville's own superhero—Pinkagirl!"

"Tonight, we're going to have a special Halloween party in Pinkville Park. Wear your costumes, and bring your candy, your pink-o'-lanterns, and your flashlights," I said. "Power or no power, we're going to make this town glow!"

My message went out over the airwaves. I hoped that everyone in town had heard it.

When Mommy and I got home, Daddy and Peter were already busy carving the pink-o'-lanterns. "It's party time!" Peter said, grinning.

Mommy and I gathered up all of the candles and flashlights we could find. Then we made some decorations. I was having lots of fun getting ready for the party with my family, but I couldn't ignore the funny feeling in my tummy. I was nervous. Was anyone going to show up? Would I get any candy?

It was still light outside when we got to the park to set up. The mayor and her family were already there, with their pink-o'-lanterns and snacks.

"Pink or treat! Pink or treat! Give us something pink to eat," Peter and I said to the mayor.

"Both," said the mayor, handing us giant pink lollipops.

"Thank you!" we said.

We finished decorating the park just as the sun started to set.

"No one's here yet," I said anxiously.

"Let's wait and see," said Daddy.

Soon I saw something off in the distance. Faint streams of light started drifting down the streets leading to the park. It looked like ghosts were floating toward us from every direction. That's when I realized what was happening: people were carrying their lit-up pink-o'-lanterns to the park!

The park glowed with pumpkins, candles, and flashlights. Everyone was laughing, having fun, and trick-or-treating right there! My favorite librarian was reading a spooky ghost story. Someone brought music so that we could dance, and someone else turned the monkey bars into a fun house!

"Pinkagirl, you really saved the day," said the mayor. I beamed.

"Hey, Pinkalicious," said Peter, "you really are a superhero. I think everyone in Pinkville came to the Halloween party! Look at all the candy we got!"

"I know," I said. "This is the most sweetalicious Halloween ever!"